Thank you for supporting an indie author.

This was my Novella November challenge for 2023

Hopefully you enjoy

Tropes include:

Strangers to Friends

Flower Disease (Hanahaki)

Snap Shot Story Telling

Minor Character Death

Past Child Abuse/Neglect

Story One:
Arbutus

"You are the only one I love"

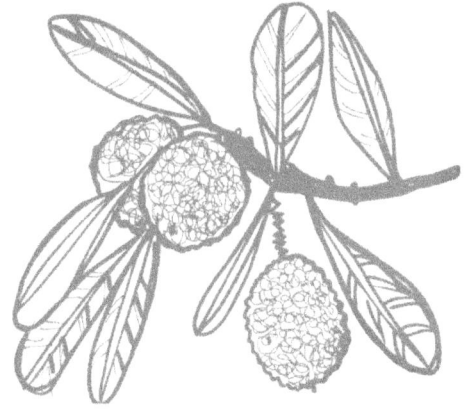

The first time that Saxon saw the red-haired elf the man was sitting alone in a dark corner of some backwoods tavern that he had stumbled into but couldn't remember the name of or where the hell in the world they even were. Not somewhere one would traditionally think of seeing such an objectively pretty elven man. Brooding would be the best way to describe what the man was doing alone at his table, glaring down at the parchment before him, breaking up his own monotony with the disapproval of the people around him as he took breaks to watch those around him mill around. He had never seen a person so disgusted by the existence of others in a dingy backwoods tavern. It honestly made the vampire want to laugh at the oddity but he had to hold it in so as not to bring attention to himself. He would have already walked over to the interesting creature to introduce himself and gain a story for a moment away from the boredom but something told him to stay where he was.

It didn't take long for a hulking figure of a human to saunter over to the elf's table without any regard for the expression on the man's face. It was obvious, at least to the hunter, that the walking wall of muscle was the local blacksmith. The man was on a mission and if Saxon couldn't damn near smell the fear on the blacksmith he would have thought he would need to step in to protect the elf from some sort of bigot. The red-haired man couldn't even look surprised as the human stopped at his table, he only looked more annoyed like he was expecting something like this. Saxon

3

himself hung to the shadows as he had been and watched, trying to get close enough to hear the hushed conversation over the noisy patrons of the bar.

"Sir, are you the poet?" The large darker man asked in a hushed whisper. It was almost too quiet for even a vampire to hear.

"Depends on who is asking and why you are asking." The elven man's voice was strained with clear frustration but still held the levity that his kind always did.

"I have the disease of flowers, sir." The man's voice dropped into a sullen tone, as it should in the man's opinion. The disease of flowers was a magical plague. The vampire sucked in a breath at the thought, feeling not pity but sympathy for the human. Saxon himself had lost a few people in his long life to that particular horror. The redhead apparently did not have the same reverence for the disease or empathy for the human.

"And so you came to a strange man in a bar?" The elf scoffed with a raised brow. Saxon nodded along knowing the elf had a point.

"You have a reputation." The human who was so large looked like a scolded child who didn't want to admit he took a frivolous risk with a stranger.

"And what reputation is that?" The redhead challenged. Saxon could see the fire in the man and he was drawn in like a moth, he was entertaining. "What rumors made you think to walk up to me as a stranger in a tavern whom you have not even confirmed my identity with."

"You are the elven poet are you not? The master poet Lord Arlen Yesvea. Greatest wordsmith of our time and the most sought-after professor of the Icbel Academy. The generous Duke overseeing the duchy of Rysiam. And most importantly the one expert on the flower disease." Saxon had to stop himself from whistling at the sheer number of titles this one elf carried on his shoulders.

"That is an impressive list. I swear you all keep adding to it for the most inane things." The elf sighed, finally setting down his ale in defeat. "I would like to make a record of the fact I only agreed to the titles of Lord, Professor, and Master Poet. Honestly, the title of Duke is too much when I travel."

"So you are him, Lord Alren." The human looked back up at the man in hope. The elve's bright purple eyes went wide in dismay.

"You weren't even positive who you were speaking to when you waltzed up to me and unloaded very private information to a stranger." The redhead hissed.

"Well…" The human looked down again, not wanting to meet the irate fire in the elve's eyes. "There are not many red-haired elves in the world and I saw you reading to the children earlier, your own poetry. I figured the chances were in my favor." Saxon was once again impressed with the human's confidence and fearlessness. Not many would be able to divulge such a secret on even a loved one and yet here he was with a stranger hoping for the best. Though, the vampire thought, how much was confidence and how much was desperation? Though talking back to such an irate person let alone a Lord, no let alone a poet was a feat of bravery all on its own.

"I suppose you have me there." The elf deflated back into his chair. "But I will be clear that I do not see where that drivel about me being an expert about anything other than turning a phrase came from." He sighed again, taking a long dreg from his mug.

"Praise spreads when you help so many people with the same problem." The larger man smirked looking back to the smaller one once more. The elf seemed to gain a dusting of color across his cheeks which only made the man smile wider.

"Slander all of it." He hissed, setting his mug down harder than necessary.

"Praise and gratitude are not slander my Lord. They are proof that you care about people, even those who are not under your sworn care."

"You are not going to leave me in peace until I assist you are you?" The elf sounded completely resigned to the idea. As though he had been backed into this very corner multiple times and knew the outcome.

"As much as I would like to give you peace, I am in true need of your help. I don't know how much longer I have before the effects truly start. I have started coughing up full flowers and that is the beginning of the end." The larger man pleaded. He was not wrong, everyone knew that when the full flowers come the affected only have a few options left before the cure consumes them. They can choose to take a chance with their beloved but even then they can only be cured or they can die. Once the full flowers emerge from the lungs, treatment from mages is no longer an option.

"Fine, I will see what I can do to help you. But we will talk tonight, somewhere more private." The elf sighed once more.

"We can meet at my workshop after closing. I can have payment and food for the inconvenience." The man said excitedly.

"The workshop will be fine, when will you close for the evening?"

"Typically I close to the public at dusk but tonight I can close the whole shop down early."

"If I am to be forced to interact with this thrice-damned disease then that should work."

"Thank you so much, my Lord. You could quite literally be saving my life." The man bowed before the elf who just waved him off.

"You very well know you could have saved yourself before this, with never bringing me into this dilemma of yours."

"I would rather lose my ability to forge steel than lose my love for him." He said with a resolve that Saxon felt damn near in his bones. Though the man seated at the table was not as moved, instead his eyes hardened for a different reason if the tension in his face was anything to go by.

"Just like everyone else willing to die because of love. You would rather die than tell them or let them go. In my own opinion that is throwing away your life."

"Then you have seen too much tragedy in your long life. But do you know what it is like? I will wait for your assistance which I will always appreciate no matter how it ends. But please do not talk ill of people who refuse to give up love. For some of us, it is the only thing we have to get us through this life." With the closure of his passionate yet discreet speech, Saxon watched as the human walked out of the tavern with the same determination that he walked in with, but just maybe more hope in his gait.

"You had no good reason to watch that like it was some sort of play for your amusement." The elf spoke in a cold tone, his gaze slowly finding the vampire who had inadvertently hidden in the shadows of the tavern.

"I didn't know you had noticed me," Saxon said as he walked towards those icy violet eyes, refusing to look at the elf directly.

"You are hard to miss, especially reeking of blood like you are." The man kicked the chair across from him out, gesturing at the vampire to sit in a way he had not offered the human. Effectively taking away an easy escape. Never before had the bounty hunter been so afraid of a sitting man, a poet nonetheless.

"If you could smell me all the way over here you have been around too much blood in your life."

"If you overheard that conversation you would know the answer to that even inadvertently." The man raised a sharp eyebrow.

"Are you going to help him?" The raven asked, finally sitting with the redhead.

"I don't want to."

"Yes, you do." The vampire leaned forward studying the man who was more interesting than anything else in this backwoods tavern. More interesting than anything he has seen in the last few decades. "I don't know you but I can tell you are the kind of man who can be forced to do something you do not want to do, especially with a sob story or righteous motive." The vampire smirked. Though his smirk damn near dropped with the hard glare he received at the light-hearted accusation.

"You are right. You do not know me." Came a cold tone to match the icy stare.

"Maybe I would like to get to know you, though I don't think I will be proven wrong about that particular observation." Saxon continued to smirk, flirting was as easy as breathing to the walking relic. The man across sat up a little straighter at the challenge.

"Flattery will get you nowhere with me." The elf shot back as if in reflex.

"Not trying to flatter you per se master poet. I am trying to see how interesting of a person you actually are to have such popularity and yet such a lack of decorum to have such an open disdain for a horrible disease that is founded in symbolism." Saxon pushed.

"Trying your own hand in poetry, are you master vampire?" The elf challenged back.

"When you are as old as I am you pick up a few skills here and there." He shrugged. "U would never be called a master such as yourself at least not in the art of words."

"And again with the flattery." The elf sighed once more. The other smiled again. "To answer your question though would not be an answer to give to a stranger in a dingy tavern with piss for ale."

"That was not a cryptic or intriguing answer at all." Saxon teased. "I am beginning to believe you are incredibly bad at dispelling interest."

"What are you going on about?" His eyes once more went hard at the lazy smile on the man across from him.

"You are making me want to stick around and figure you out, to see the man behind the obvious walls."

"Then you will be left with nothing but disappointment." The redhead grunted rising from his chair with all intentions of leaving the tavern alone and the conversation unfinished.

"Just a friendly warning but if you leave now I will have no choice but to follow you." He warned the standing man with a glint of mirth in his eyes and a playful smile on his face. He knew exactly what he was doing.

"I have a feeling I will be cursed with you following behind even if I were to answer all the questions you could think of. Like a sense of foreboding but I need to know why is it me who has caught your infernal interest?"

"Because you interest me, like an unknown pull or a puzzle I just can't piece together. I want to know why people come to you, and why people are drawn to you, especially in their time of need. Why were you the only one I noticed in this entire tavern of strange people?" Saxon answered.

"Are you truly so bored as to speculate like a philosopher?" The elf sighed once more before admitting defeat and retaking his seat at the table.

"Well, the easy answer is yes I am." The jovial answer made the elf raise his brow in disbelief. "The slightly longer answer is what if this interest is the fate's way of showing us something to come?"

"I don't believe in something like fate outside of a fairytale." The poet huffed.

"Ah, then my strange poet, the longest answer you can wait for until after we meet with the smithy." The vampire smirked knowing he had won.

It was just as the sun was on the horizon that the elven poet stood outside the blacksmith's shop waiting with an over-eager vampire by his side. The vampire had refused to stop babbling about absolute nonsense since leaving the tavern. His nonsense was truly about nothing of meaning but somehow everything he seemed to be able to think of. He had tried to think of anything that could lead him to any truthful answers about the elf with or without him knowing the facts he was sharing. Yet none of his insistent chatter could clue the other man on why he was so keen to follow behind on such a morbid errand. The elf was making a show of trying to ignore his companion by staring across the cobblestone street to the brick wall of the empty business that sat across from the blacksmith's workshop.

"I know that this is probably a little late to ask but are you ever going to ask my name?" The raven asked. "Or what I do? That would have been the polite thing to do wouldn't have been?"

"Why would I? After this evening you will have no reason to bother me anymore. And politeness was lost when you decided to attach yourself to my side like a leech." The redhead answered in an indifferent tone.

"Then can I know your name?" The vampire tried again.

"No, because I am not a fool." The blunt answer made the vampire stop for a moment in surprise. "High vampires, much like the fae, can use names for various reasons. Now why would I give mine willingly to a high vampire that is a stranger and smells like a battlefield?" Saxon was impressed with an elf of all to know such secrets of vampire culture.

"As impressed as I am that you know that tidbit of knowledge and it is a good idea to typically follow, I would like to add that not all of us have the power of names. Though I am curious about how you know that and how you could tell I was a higher vampire of all things." The larger man mused. "But also it is not the power of names one has to truly worry about, it is the power of blood."

"Do not worry about what I may or may not know or how I know it. I am well aware of the power of blood, never let a vampire you do not know and trust heal you" The elf shrugged nonchalantly.

"Though I have to agree with you it seems like you do not trust vampires, or fae for that matter." The vampire prodded.

"I do not trust many, there is no reason to I have found. Many die before they are worthy of trust and the rest are simply not worth trusting, simple as that." It was one shock after another with this man. Saxon had never met such a truly distanced elf before. From those he knew and from what he knew elves were a very social culture and species. Needing affection and expression even if that expression was anger and venom. They were one of the most, not open, but expressive and social creatures on the planet. Some truly thought that without affection and attention much like their fae relatives they would perish. He had never met one so shielded and cold.

"Have you no long living friends or relations?"

"Again with your pointless interest." Saxon was beginning to believe sighing was a hobby for this elf. He would be worried about the dramatics if the other was not a poet, the only thing worse would have been a bard.

"I will remind you it is not pointless for someone who is honestly trying to get to know you." Saxon pushed back, feeling strangely defensive at the comment.

"Don't waste the effort. You won't be around long enough to learn anything of importance." The elf looked over at the vampire for a brief moment before returning to looking at the blank brick of the building across the cobblestone street from where they leaned.

"You are surely underestimating my ability to be interested in someone. I have lived long enough to know when someone could be worth sticking around for." The elf scoffed at the idea.

"Don't bother, as I already told you, you will not be seeing me again if luck is on your side." Before Saxon could respond the heavy door of the workshop finally opened.

"I am sorry gentlemen. I needed to finish up a project before I could air out the heat from the forge." The blacksmith apologized, wiping the soot and oil from his hands. If he was surprised at all about the second man standing beside the poet he asked assistance from he did not show it at all.

"No problems at all, my good man. You have a business to run and we respect that." Saxon stepped forward in front of the elf who was still leaning against the brick with his arms crossed around his middle, clearly uncomfortable. "My apologies for not being able to introduce myself earlier." He smiled, reaching his hand out for the man. He could smell the anxiety coming off the elf now that they were once more in front of the blacksmith who needed his assistance, now that the smell was not covered with ale and sweat.

"Understandable good sir." The blacksmith reached to shake hands with the vampire's hand in a strong grip for a human. "In your defense, I did ambush Lord Alren earlier in the tavern. I am Iohn Bar, nothing more than the simple blacksmith in this town."

"Saxon Veinir." The vampire replied. "And you already know my Lordly counterpart here."

"Do not introduce me." The elf hissed, finally pushing himself off the wall. His reaction only caused the other man to chuckle.

"Yes, his reputation certainly precedes him." The human answered with a gentle smile.

"Let us go inside and get this over with," Alren grumbled. "Let us at least actually go into the building so we are no longer looking suspicious as we loiter outside the business."

"Yes please, welcome to my shop. I do apologize I was not able to prepare food beforehand since some commissions came in late with a short deadline." Iohn smiled even wider as he walked the two visitors into his workspace. Saxon could not see anything remarkable in the smithy's workspace, nothing that would truly stand out. Not that he expected to find a gem in this backwater town but he could tell the pride the man had in his work and the vampire would never think to diminish it.

"Do you know who you have flowers for?" Alren spoke bluntly as soon as the door was locked behind them. Straight to the point much to Saxon's growing amusement with the man.

"Sir Ywain, a knight for the Count that looks over our town. He is a sweet and gentle man." Iohn spoke clearly in love, which he would need to be with his affliction. It didn't take long for that soft smile and obvious pinning to lead to violent coughing taking hold of the otherwise sturdy man. It pained the older vampire to see such a young and healthy man bent in half struggling to breathe, choking quite literally on his own feelings. Part of him hoped the elf would help quickly with this magic-made illness. The raven-haired vampire watched in slight horror as the coughing stopped and the human stayed bent over wheezing, holding the bloodied flowers that escaped him in his hands.

"When you can breathe again, hand me the buds. You are far enough along that you will have your answer. However, then you can only choose which path you are willing to take. And you will have to choose before the roots take hold and choose for you."

"As I said earlier I will not remove them by force. I can not lose what happiness I have. Without him, I am alone here. I am an outsider in this town, an outsider who was chased from their home for something I had nothing to do with." Iohn forced out with a trembling voice.

"What happened if you don't mind telling us," Saxon asked carefully, stepping closer to the large man in case he needed help. The human didn't speak again until the older man helped lead him to a nearby chair, finally unable to stop the urge to get the unsteady man more balanced. Once he is seated by his own hearth he seems to be able to take full breaths again.

"A girl in my village got the flowers because of my first love, a farmer's son. When she died they blamed it on us. They chased me out and last I heard murdered him in cold-blooded retribution." Tears streamed down his face. "I ran as far as I could and tried to live a solitary life. I have tried to stay away from everyone who could cause me pain. Maybe this is my punishment for what happened to her."

"How would either of you need to get punished for valid feelings that frankly had nothing to do with you in one way or another. It was her choice." Alren sighed again stepping towards the man, Saxon watched as the elf's demeanor softened. "She made her choice just as you need to make yours. Don't think your brief happiness is not possibly worth the pain and the peace that it will bring you. If it is true then it will be worth it in the end." He said much gentler than the vampire expected. The elf opened the human's hands and looked intently at the flowers that resided within.

"Why are we cursed for loving someone?" The man sobbed.

"No one knows. I choose to think of it not as a curse but as your feelings are so true and deep, like a pool, that something beautiful must grow. We are just not made to hold that kind of depth and feeling trapped in such a delicate vessel."

"Such pretty words. No wonder you are a master poet." The man smiled again finally, tears still flowing as he watched the elven man.

"You are truly lucky though." The redhead spoke carefully looking away from the human and towards the delicate flower in his large callused hands. "This is an arbutus bloom."

"What does that mean?" Saxon could only call the man's words a whimper, the hope was almost too much to be contained in the man's large body.

"The loose translation is 'You are the only one I love'. But the message is there. Meaning you need to talk to your knight very soon."

"You could be cured tonight." Saxon encouraged the shocked man in the chair. "How far away is he?" He pressed.

"Down the street." He choked out looking at the vampire in complete disbelief. His eyes were large and in complete shock.

"Then go to him." Alren pushed, making the human look back at him. "We can lock the door, go to him, and free yourself." The man finally snapped into action, scrambling from the chair and out the door. He didn't even bother to close the front door once he had fought with the lock and made it back to the street. The two remaining men looked at each other and sighed in unison. Saxon reached his hand out to help the elf up from his knelt position. His hands were more calloused than Saxon expected. They moved in complete silence as they walked towards the open door in time to see the blacksmith talking shyly to an impossibly longer man. It didn't take long for the two humans to hug each other, obviously incredibly emotional.

"They will get their happy ending." Saxon smiled, taking a chance to take a look at the elf next to him. His expression was something the vampire could not describe if he wanted to.

"That really depends on them. Nothing is ever guaranteed." The way he said it intrigued the bounty hunter even more. Something about his tone cried out something that pulled at Saxon but he couldn't quite put his finger on it.

"You are only interesting me more master poet." He warned.

"And you are already irritating me, but alas soon you will be nothing but a memory instead of a thorn." The elf sighed, his face once more going completely impassive, losing the soft qualities that it possessed before.

"You underestimate me Lord Alren Yesven." The elf flinched at his name coming from the vampire's mouth. "We will both have a long time and I am not done with you yet." Groaning the man walked away only to have the other follow, knowing this would go somewhere very interesting. Almost as if he could feel their own story take root.

Story Two:
Asphodel

"My regrets follow you to the grave."

Months had followed that no-name town and Saxon laughed every time he saw the elven poet after. They would meet in the strangest locations on the continent for various reasons and only stay together a few days before the poet would inevitably disappear. This particularly rainy morning as Saxon dragged himself into a city with a large manor and a rogue vampire in need of dispatching he could not believe his good fortune as he trudged up to the city wall and he spotted the distinguishing red hair that he adored to tease about so much. He could see that auburn hair through the low fog that came with the nonstop drizzle that had plagued the area for days on end. Before he could make himself a nuisance to the other man like he normally loved to do every time his eyes landed on the elf he noticed a peculiar scene that made him stop in his tracks. The noble was not alone, instead, he stood beside a man and a woman, human from where he was standing, and the elf had a gentle smile proudly on his face. The vampire had yet to see such a soft and open expression on the poet's face before now. The man and woman seemed to be happy even though they were leaving the poet to continue on their way. Behind their hugs and waves goodbye the gentle smile turned into soft sadness that Saxon could not stand seeing. His counterpart obviously cherished these two humans. As silently as possible the vampire stalked forward, behind the elf, needing more information about his closed-off acquaintance.

"And here, my dear Lord, I thought you didn't have any friends," Saxon whispered into Alren's ear as soon as he stood directly behind him. It earned him the most beautiful and undignified squeak he could have ever wished for. Saxon could not keep himself from doubling over in laughter as they started beating on him repeatedly with a book that had been in his hands and he had managed not to drop in his fright. "That bodes well for me then Mr I-don't-get-attached" He smiled, eyes full of mischief, as he stood back up to his full height. Red dusted the elf's entire face.

"You are a vile infection that refuses to stay gone from me." Alren hisses continuing to hit the vampire who was still grinning like a maniac. It took a moment for them both to calm down and for Saxon to appreciate the shift in their relationship. In the last six months, the shift was more than the vampire could have predicted. Even if the elf swore that he thought the vampire was a leech that would not stay gone, Though that analogy was a bit on the nose for his liking. The poet couldn't hide how relaxed whenever the hunter was around. Saxon never brought it up to keep the posturing down.

However, this time was different when the scent of blood came from the elf as he moved around. The moment the scent registered with the vampire he stopped and glanced over the elf to see for any visible wounds on the man before him. He could not find anything visible, but that wasn't saying much with the amount of layers the nobleman wore.

"Alren, I need you to be honest with me for a moment." His change of tone caught the poet's attention immediately.

"That depends on if you are about to ask me something asinine again. The last time you asked me if I ever wrote erotica about inbreeding nobles that I personally knew." He shot back clearly worrying about the sudden change in mood.

"Are you injured?"

"Why do you ask?" Alren asked, tensing ever so slightly. If not for his training the rave-haired man would have missed it.

"You smell of blood." He answered honestly with a raised brow, something was truly strange with the reaction. Not as someone who was bleeding by a vampire but as someone who is hiding information. Alren had to know he would notice. He was a vampire for fucks sake.

"Don't worry about it. It is nothing life-threatening and already under control." Obviously forcing himself to relax in front of the hunter.

"If you are sure. I can look at it for you if you need, or I know some amazing healers." Saxon insisted not at all liking the implication of the poet not taking care of himself.

"Calm yourself you fool. Now are you planning to follow me around this city like a lost pup you tend to be?" The elf smirked knowing the vampire truly loathed being treated like a lycan. Saxon knew the man was just trying to get a rise out of him to distract him from his line of questions. The vampire let it go since the smell of blood had left the elf as suddenly as it had come.

"Why do you insist on treating me like a dog?" He sighed dramatically, throwing his head back. They both knew it didn't bother the larger man nearly as much as he acted but it was part of the way they danced around each other.

"Why do YOU insist on acting like a stray coming to heel for an unwilling master? And I haven't even fed you." He teased finally relaxing truly again stepping towards the entrance to the city with one last look to where the humans had walked off to. Saxon knew better than to ask about them quite yet if his earlier reaction was anything.

"I mean if that is how we build our relationship from stray to companion I will gladly accept you feeding me." Saxon retorted suggestively causing a surprised laugh to come from the elf.

"Then I would truly never get a break from you." He shook his head as they crossed the threshold. He had no doubt that the hunter was silently only a step behind him. "Never again would I have a moment of peace."

"You are writing prose about me again little lordling." Saxon teased as he followed the elf with no concern into the hospitality district.

"Oh hush you, just because you are a behemoth of a beast does not mean anything." Alren shot back walking towards one of the taverns lining the dirt street.

"It means you are tiny and still have too many titles for one man." Saxon teased back as he stepped forward to open the door for the smaller male.

"You just have no culture you heathen. And just for that, you can buy the first inevitable round of the evening." The man smirked, looking at his companion with mischief in his eyes. It didn't take long for Saxon to learn he would never win when the elf looked at him like that.

"Be careful with my purse lordling otherwise you will be the one paying for our lodgings while I work this contract." He replied with a wink as they walked to the bar in sync. Anyone on the outside would think they had a much longer and deeper relationship than a spotty six months of hit-or-miss meetings.

"Like you won't bully your way into my room drunk off your ass." The else sighed finally looking at the vampire beside him. "What is the contract this time?" He asked carefully.

"Do not worry it just sounds like a lower race of vampire is committing far too many murders in the city walls. Too reckless and cocksure for a higher race for sure. My thought is possibly newly turned. Shouldn't be too difficult but should take down fairly easily though it will be a night or two to track. No need to worry Alren." Saxon responded by lowering his voice. "I have been doing this a long time."

"I am not worried." The poet bit back but the scent of anxiety had been rolling off him since the hunter mentioned the contract. The vampire had to hold back a smile. Alren was trying so hard to pretend he was completely unattached to all, but like every other poet in the land, he felt deeply and could only pretend for so long.

"If you say so."

"I was just wondering since I will be here a few days reading poetry at the manor and the local library." The elf sighed trying to play the part. "I was just trying to plan how much of a nuisance you will be during my stay."

"You know one day I will get you to admit you like me even a little bit," Saxon smirked gently pushing Alren playfully, he didn't even move.

"Only in your dreams you leech." He answered with a small smirk.

"We have an eternity for me to work you down to admit you have feelings that are not just on paper."

"I need to find a way to avoid you permanently."

"Not even in death my good poet." He laughed, causing his partner to sigh loudly as always. "Excuse me barkeep can we have two ales down here at our end?" The vampire finally called out. He watched the elf shake his head fondly and walk to an empty table towards the corner. Once he had their drinks he sauntered over to where the poet was lounging where he sat. "How does one lounge in a tavern chair?" He asked.

"Your imagery is always impeccable. I am not lounging." The elf opened his vibrant purple eyes as the vampire sat down the tankards on the wooden table. He chuckled as he sat across from the other.

"You are thinking in poetry again aren't you?" Saxon chuckled looking at the almost lazy look on the poet's face. It was the look the hunter became familiar with right before he fell face first in paper and words. The younger man suspected the scent of paper and ink was permanently embedded in the elf.

"I have no idea what you are going on about."

"You are just mad at how fast I have been able to read you." Saxon teased.

"You don't know what you are talking about." Alren sighed once more.

"So you are not going to spend your free time writing another masterpiece or two while in the city?"

"Hush you." He hissed again.

"I knew it. When are your readings?" He tried distracting the elf before he lost him to his musings.

"Oh once in the morning at the manor and then another in the late afternoon at the city library. Starting tomorrow, I will go for four days. I will be gone again by the end of the week."

"So I have plenty of time to fulfill my contract and catch a few readings before you rush off into the night like a noncommittal lover." That earned him a kick to the leg. "Are we not sharing a room?" He laughed as the elf groaned, tossing his head back. When he sat back up he took a long gulp of the ale.

They ended up having to share a room thankfully with two beds. Since there was such a crowd hoping to hear Alren read his poetry. Saxon laughed at his companion's face when they were told, in complete shock and dismay. The elf kept grumbling and downright pouting as the hunter unpacked his little travel belongings. Saxon kept reassuring him he would barely be in the room until the contract was done so Alren could write to his heart's content without interruption other than his readings. Not that this was the first time they have shared a room before let alone while inspiration held the poet in its control. And like that the days went smoothly, pretending to not notice the worried smell from the elf every time he returned to the room until the newly turned vampire was dead. He also allowed the elf to act aloof even when he was checking the hunter over for injuries and making sure he was healthy. Saxon knew better than to take the aloof act as it looked. His walls just made the vampire wonder what could have caused such a social creature like an elf to be so completely closed off to relationships and affection.

They had both been relaxing in their room, Saxon was just cleaning his various weapons and Alren sat at the desk writing away too far off in his own world. The calm and domestic feel in the room was broken by a sudden knock at the door breaking both of their concentration and startling them. Call him paranoid but he shot from his spot on the floor and to the door long before the poet could even stand from his chair. He knew logically that Alren was a dangerous person in his own way and could protect himself but Saxon was much harder to kill. He heard the man sigh behind him and mumble something about 'overprotective brutes' but paid absolutely no mind to the redhead. They had been subject to multiple crazed fans in their tentative friendship, some who would not take a no from the man and some who wanted to genuinely hurt the poet. None of those situations were acceptable for the vampire and he did not want any repeats. Though the lack of apprehension from the elf scared him more, it was terrifying to think of how often this could happen when the vampire was elsewhere. Slowly and cautiously he opened the door completely blocking the frame and more importantly blocking the elf from sight. What met him was a small and seemingly innocent woman with a determined look in her dark eyes.

"You are not the poet." She said sternly and with no fear of the large man in front of her. A younger half-elf if Saxon had to guess with her white hair, fair complexion, and most importantly small pointed ears much shorter than his traveling companion.

"No, I am not and you are a stranger." He answered in a low and level voice showing off his fangs more than strictly necessary. Just because she didn't seem a threat didn't mean she wasn't full of unpleasant surprises. He did his best to ignore the sigh from behind him but he knew any posturing would come to an end as he heard the poet get up from his chair and leaving the safety of the provided desk. Saxon didn't even flinch as he felt a gentle hand on his back noting the elf's arrival behind him. The small forms of physical touch had been new the first time Saxon stepped in between him and a jealous scholar who had never gotten their own works published. Saxon had almost lost his composure entirely when he saw the dagger in the elf's side from someone who the poet said was a colleague. He had only calmed when Alren let him stitch him up and kept touching him saying he would not die so easily. Now the small touches were grounding and full of unsaid understanding.

"Move you brute," Alren said pushing Saxon out of the way, his words harsher than his touch so the vampire allowed it. Saxon didn't like the idea of not standing in between Alren and the unknown woman but he had to trust his companion. Not that he didn't just step behind the smaller man to make sure there was not a replay of history. The frequency of incidents was the real reason that they continued to share a room whenever they were together no matter how much each bitched about it, feeling safer together. The vampire was unimpressed by how he had become familiar with the scent of the elf's blood. "I must apologize, my dear," he said looking at the woman, sounding as charming as he always did at first. "He is a bit protective for some unknown reason. How may I help you?"

"He is a good friend to be so cautious of your callers, especially with your fame and rank my Lord. I can only imagine the horrors that you have opened your door to completely unaware. Though I may ask that we step inside before I divulge why I am here. I have a delicate request wrapped in a complicated set of circumstances." She asked quieting her voice, periodically looking up and down the hall to make sure no one was listening.

"Are you sure you wish to come in my lady? Wouldn't it be improper for you to enter the room of two men, two strangers?" The poet insisted, watching how the woman fidgeted in the hall clearly uncomfortable.

"No one will think otherwise but thank you. This will be quick and then I will leave and not worry about the words of this city anyway." She nodded pushing her way into the room, completely uncaring of the condition of the room or the men in front of her. Turning to face them she held her hand out to the redhead revealing a delicate flower in her palm. "I only need to know about this." Saxon saw the way the poet's eyes darkened knowing once more exactly what the flower was. Not even the vampire needed to be able to smell the blood on the petals to know what this was about.

"You have the flower disease and you think I can help you." He answered instead, his voice dropping all charm in the same way it did the first time in that no-name tavern and every other time someone has asked since. Saxon was beginning to truly hate this tone, he still felt sympathy for those asking for help but no longer thought the price for the poet was worth it.

"No, I need to know what it means before I make my final decision on what to do. I do not want any what-ifs to follow me in my path. I know a lot about the disease, my human mother died from it when my elven father was ushered away to somewhere more acceptable for his station and did not put up a fight. Now I have it and even though I have elven blood in my veins it can kill me if I do not take action."

"May I ask who it is for?" Saxon asked carefully, feeling like they were owed the story since they had been dragged in.

"My Lady of the Manor since I can be honest here. I think I know it is a meaningless endeavor and have already have plans to seek out a mage when we are done here. And if that is the case after I will leave without a word and no one the wiser. But as I said I need to be certain, if there is some hope then I need to know so I do not give up this feeling so easily."

"Asphodel means 'my regrets follow you to the grave', hopefully, that is the answer you need even if not the one you want," Alren responded quietly. The woman sighed heavily.

"I had a feeling it was going to be something like that." She chuckled without humor. Saxon watched as she deflated with defeat, no longer being the strong and determined woman who had stood before him in the doorway. Now she stood like a lost child who had her world shifted irrevocably. "She told me feelings don't matter when titles are in question. She offered to enjoy each other and to be her dirty secret that she kept in the shadows. But I would never have her heart nor her hand since I was just a lowly maid. If I had been born someone important then maybe there would have been different options for us."

"What do titles have to do with anything?" Saxon huffed aloud without thinking.

"Some noble families don't accept same-sex couples but more likely she is planning on trying to marry up and become more than the lady of a manor. She is hoping to climb the noble ladder and have more power, more prestige." Alren replied to him without ever taking his eyes off the woman.

"You are not wrong unfortunately, she has always wanted more. She is ambitious and that is something I love about her but I think she is looking for more in the wrong way. But again I am just a maid so my concern means nothing." She sighed once more, wrapping her arms around herself, her fist once again clenched around the flower. Though Saxon was relieved to see she was seeming to rebuild herself right before their eyes.

"Nobles are horrible and selfish creatures. I will never understand them." Saxon spit before noticing a raised brow directed at him from his companion. "Of course, the present company and his family are excluded. My lordling whom I absolutely cherish his companionship and his art." The elf hummed before looking back at the half elf before them who was clearly watching their exchange with amusement.

"Ignoring the idiot in the room, have you made your choice with confidence?"

"Yes, as I have said I have sought out a mage already. My things were packed in preparation for this. As I said earlier I had no real hope but I needed to be certain. I will be done and out of the city by nightfall."

"You didn't have even an ounce of hope and you still could not give her up with assistance? Knowing all of what you have told us?" Alren asked as though he was honestly confused by her position.

"Sometimes your head and your heart can not agree no matter what you do." She answered. "Sometimes it is ok to ask for help when you can't be strong enough to do what is good for you alone. And that could be to either hold on or to let go." She answered. "But I must thank you for your assistance and for the chance to say it all aloud. I will have to take my leave now gentlemen." And with the same determination she walked in with she left. Saxon looked over to his counterpart as he stepped closer to the door.

"Are you alright?" He asked gently once again unsure of what to make of the expression on the poet's face.

"I don't think I will ever truly understand people with this curse. Or how they come to their decisions. Or worse yet how I play into it."

"I don't think one person is meant to understand it all. Each person has their own story, their own fears, and their own reasons." The vampire tried. "You bring some clarity to the people who come to you and give them the strength to hold on or to let go."

"How do I give that to others when I can not do that for myself." He mumbled before going back to the desk and his papers without another explanation. They both stayed silent for the rest of the night.

Saxon watched from the crowd as Alren read his last set of poetry that he was paid to read in this city. There were plenty of people within the library trying to get one last moment to hear the master speak his own work. The raven noticed that the fiery elf had chosen some of his more somber pieces, most thought it was the way he did his farewell reading but the man knew better. He had watched his counterpart become more subdued after the maid had left without a second thought or even her name the night before. Alren was as mesmerizing as always but there was another who had caught the vampire's attention this evening. The lady of the manor herself had also come to the library to sit and listen with her people. The brunette woman had seemed more sullen than she had been the entire time they had been in the city walls. Saxon had a feeling he knew exactly why the woman seemed more distressed and hollow than the days before, regrets in the form of petals his mind supplied. He had spent too much time listening to Alren rework prose again. For the maid asking for help, he could not stay silent and not intervene. She had to know what she lost in her ignorance and arrogance. He could not let others get hurt in the same way if he could help it.

"My Lady Jalia," he greeted her. "How are you doing this afternoon? Are you not enjoying Lord Alren's works? You seem to have something troubling you." He asked, sounding genuinely concerned, slightly startling her.

"Oh Sir Saxon, I apologize I did not see you. I must be trapped in my thoughts. Please don't mind me, I am feeling a bit melancholy today." She tried to smile but it just came across tired.

"Care to share your burden? I would never leave someone in a state of melancholy without a way to ease it if I can." He pushed watching her think of it for a moment.

"My companion Milani left without a word. She took everything and left last night with no explanation or warning." She forced out in obvious pain. Saxon was proud of the maid, Milani, had followed through with her plan, and that it worked.

"You do not know why?" He asked.

"I honestly don't. I thought I had given her everything she could want, compromising with our positions. There is no reason I can think of for her to leave."

"Now I do not know much about the situation but maybe it was not everything she could want. Maybe the answer was simple and now it is something you will regret."

"What do you mean?" She asked, confused.

"Sometimes titles do not matter as much as the matters of the heart." He shrugged before walking back over to the elf who was waiting for him. The lady left in shock and horror at the implication as the poet asked what the man was smirking about now. The vampire placated the man as he led him back out of the library since the reading was over. He wanted them both out of the city before they were asked more about the missing woman.

Story Three:
Alcea Rosea

"Please Remember Me"

     Seasons passed and time doesn't stop no matter who wishes it would. In a blink of an eye, another year had passed before Saxon got Alren to greet him without fake disdain when they happened upon each other. He knew their relationship had grown surprisingly fast since they met. The frequency of dire or emotional situations played into the growth, though Saxon also hoped part of it was Alren's natural need to reach out with his elven blood. Most of the growth had been the unique situation and the heavy burden of people continuously asking for help that the poet did not want to provide. Every time the hunter was not surprised that the poet caved and helped, seeming to hurt himself in the process each and every time, leaving the larger man to try and pick up the pieces that he could find. He would take guarding the elf from crazed fans and the redhead sewing him back together after a bad hunt any day over people showing up with flowers.

     This time the two had actually planned to meet since Alren had a competition that he was competing in. Saxon had all but demanded to play bodyguard at all events like this after a few more attempts on the lord's life. The elf had taken to just bringing the events up in casual conversation or their spotty correspondence instead of dealing with the aftermath of Saxon not being informed or gods forbid the aftermath of his blood being spilled again.

"I haven't been in Hyluc in ages, maybe a few decades at least." Saxon groaned, stretching out on the lounge in the sitting room. "Why am I not surprised you have a small house in such a historic city."

"I do teach at the college, Icbel Academy, at least one season out of the year, I am here every winter at least." The elf side-eyed him from his chair in front of the fireplace.

"I forgot you winter here and not in Rysiam." Saxon shrugged, Alren seemed surprised that he remembered the name of his lands but made no comment.

"I winter here and I travel to Rysiam in the spring since it is close by. During the spring I have to deal with things like crops, taxes, repairs, and all the other unimpressive things that go into a duchy. Then I let my council led by Bylar help through the rest of the year. They can always easily get a hold of me or find me if I am needed but we tend to have peace in our lands. However, I do step home when I can through the year and surprise everyone. I was actually there before meeting you here this year." Alren explained surprising Saxon by willingly giving a bit more of himself up than normal.

"I winter at Tybia with my family but normally I travel as you know. The glamorous life of a bounty hunter."

"If I may, how did you even end up in this life? You don't seem like the kind who wanted to try to hunt down the monsters across the continent."

"Oh, that is not as impressive of a story as one would hope. When I was young I killed a rogue vampire, I was protecting some people in an ambush. After the story spread I was recruited to the hunters guild." He sighed not really wanting to go too far into the story, it was not a memory he liked to think of. The blood, the fear, and the feeling of going feral for the first time were all ingrained in him in a way that still caused nightmares.

"Always trying to be a hero even when you were little. Always having to protect those around you even when you could get seriously hurt. And you say I have little self-preservation." Alren chided softly. The atmosphere was calm and relaxed. Saxon was surprised, he had been glorified since the day it happened but never had he been called a hero in such a way. "How old were you?"

"Maybe 120 years old. Barely out of childhood and in my adolescence."

"I am truly not surprised it started so young. How old are you now?" Alren pushed, surprising Saxon again.

"Normally I would make a comment about being rude and never asking a lady's age.."

"But you are no lady." The elf teased with a straight face, not giving into the vampire's shenanigans visibly.

"First excuse you, I am a lady of the finest caliber, and second of all I am not missing the opportunity of you actually asking more questions about me. I am a young 1168 years old, born and raised in the Keep of Tybia with the other northern higher vampires."

"Oh, you are much younger than I expected. I thought you might be younger than me but not by that much." Alren said as an afterthought of shock before shaking his head and going back to his book.

"How are you in shock at my age?" Saxon asked mildly concerned. "How old are you Alren?"

"Only 1556 years old. Though that does mean I am a full three centuries older than you plus a little." He answered not looking up from the pages as the vampire had to rethink what he thought he knew. Saxon honestly thought that the elf was younger than him, smaller and younger. But no the man had more than three centuries on him of life. "338 years to be exact if my math is correct."

"You are almost four centuries older than me." He wheezed out.

"It would seem so. Why are you upset by this?" Alren looked over with a raised brow.

"I am not upset I am shocked." He admitted. "I figured you were younger than me for some reason. And to find out you are that much older than me."

"In our long lives, it is not that much. I was still a child when you were born if that makes you feel better."

"Do not lie to me you were almost a young adult by then if I know elven lives as well as I think I do."

"Fine, you are right I was in fact a young adult when you were born." He sighed, laying his book in his lap. "Not that it matters much in a lifespan like ours. We might not be truly immortal but we are damn close."

"When did you take over your duchy?" Saxon pushed his luck trying to get more information since Alren was in such a talkative mood.

"I believe I was just shy of 700 years old. I know my sister was turning 500 the same year so I had to have been 688." Alren looked thoughtful as if trying to honestly remember. "I only remember because 500 was a big accomplishment in our culture. And since our father is a lower prince, low enough to never see the crown not that the old man or any of us really care. But it does put us part of the southern monarchy of elves,"

"You have a sister?"

"Again you focus on the strangest things. Yes, I have a younger sister, I believe I have mentioned her. Her name is Bylar and she is 188 years younger than me. Making her I believe 200 years older than you."

"You rarely talk about yourself, especially willingly. Who knew I just had to get you to invite me home with you."

"We will have been at two years of knowing each other here soon" The elf looked back at the fire instead of actually acknowledging what the other said. "You don't seem to be going away any time soon so there may be no actual harm in letting you know the basics that even the public has access to."

"Is it so hard to admit that you like me as a person and you need some damn near immortal friends outside of your sister?" Saxon sighed laying back down in frustration. He had been right, almost two full years of being beside each other as often as they could. And yet he still could not admit they were friends.

"I have been told as of recently that having very few friends is unnatural for my kind and having the few I do have being all mortal has been worrying those who have cared for me for so long. I may have received a full lecture about both subjects." Alren admitted sighing again, still looking into the fire. "I was once again pushed on why an elf such as myself is so isolated."

"Good on them. I wasn't aware I had help in my mission to wear you down and get you to open up."

"Apparently I spent this past spring complaining about you nonstop to anyone who would listen back home. I thought I was going on about what an overprotective leech you were who decided to attach yourself to me like a parasite. Apparently, I gave them the impression that I had been hiding a long-term friend that I had never brought home to meet the family. They thought I was ashamed of them or my position as a noble since we met as a hunter and a traveling poet." He sighed once more. "I then had to have the lengthy conversation that we were not in fact long-term friends nor was I ashamed of any of them. We, at the time, had barely over a year of whatever you consider this relationship of you following me around thinking I am some vulnerable bleeding heart or gods forbid lonely. They took that to mean we were quick friends and that you were some sort of miracle. That is when I received both lectures one after the other."

"And who do I owe this thanks to? If they managed to get that through your stubborn head that having friends is not some sort of punishment."

"Do not concern yourself with such details."

"So it is the humans I am not allowed to meet." The elf hummed in agreement until he coughed violently, almost dropping his book to the ground. "Are you alright? Are you allergic to feelings like I suspected?" The vampire tried to tease through the worry as the elf finally caught his breath. His normally pale skin was dusted with the pink of excursion with the force of the fit. The smell of blood wafted over to the vampire, as faint as the other times he had seen the man cough suddenly. Normally it was a small fit with the smell of blood and then both disappeared as fast as it came. Each of the handful of times the same thing occurred pain sat in the raven's chest. His friend was sick, sick enough to have blood in his lungs even with elven blood in his veins. Elven sicknesses were rare and could be incredibly dangerous to one of the most naturally immune creatures in the world.

"I have told you every time I am fine. It is being handled and though inconvenient will do no lasting damage to me." Alren said, waving the vampire off like he did every time.

"Yes, but the smell of blood I detect every time you cough like that is getting stronger. If you were not an elf I would be more concerned but it has been over a year Alren and it isn't getting better. There are only a few blood diseases that you can have and even fewer that are survivable."

"I have it handled you stubborn ass." The redhead started closing in on himself again before the vampire's very eyes."Why can you not just trust me on my own health?"

"Do not dare use this to build those walls back up Alren. Just because you have only admitted we may be friends does not mean it is a new concept for me. I have seen too much death to ignore relationships of any form, especially if they matter. And to me, ours matter. I have been too invested in you and worried about your well-being for you to shut me out the moment that you start feeling uncomfortable with someone caring, someone who might be able to stick around for the long haul." The elf looked truly shocked at the outburst. It was clearly building for quite frustrations over time.

"I am sorry for my flippant nature regarding our relationship then Saxon. I honestly did not know you felt that deeply about it or were garnering frustrations during our time so far."

"How could you not know how I felt? I never hid it." Saxon looked over at his friend feeling surprisingly hurt at the dismissal of their time and their experiences. "When have I ever made you think that I don't value our time or relationship?"

"I promise you have not. This is on me and my own burdens. Maybe I have spent too much time with mortals. I am far more used to as long as it is handled my health is not much of a concern. It is much harder to hide ailments when someone can live long enough to see the consequences of my actions. But I assure you Saxon that I am alright and my illness is being handled. It is no danger to me."

"Well do not be truly offended when you get dragged to the healer in the morning for a professional to ease my mind." Saxon sighed back again.

"Salari can't help much but if you need to know what condition I have I can tell you."

"How do I know you wouldn't try and downplay whatever it is?" Saxon didn't know why he was feeling so defensive about the topic or so hurt. "Past jokes aside, I don't know how to trust you with honesty about your own health. You barely just began to tell me about the man outside the traveling poet."

Alren watched him thoughtfully, clearly weighing his options. A long drawn-out breath brought the vampire's attention back to the elf when the coughing started again. Never had the fits been so close together. The smell of blood was slightly stronger than the last fit. Disregarding his feelings Saxon sprung back up from the lounge and rushed to the other man's side, using more speed than necessary in a confined room but his judgment was clouded by fear. Without a second thought, he fell to his knees beside the seated man so he could carefully begin to rub between the smaller man's shoulders trying to ease his discomfort. It felt like an eternity until whatever was trying to escape his lungs finally came out allowing the poet to spit it into his hands. The smell was more persistent as a small trail of blood and spit could be seen at the corner of his mouth, staining the pale skin dramatically. Saxon honestly could say at this moment he once again hated the sight of blood. Alren looked far too calm for such a violent episode. Carefully he sat back, not once mentioning the physical contact or shying away from the large hand that had stayed on his back from the man knelt beside him.

"I have honestly never tried to cause a fit on purpose before." He said with his voice hoarse, clearing his throat a time or two.

"What do you mean on purpose?" Saxon all about squawked in disbelief. Without a further explanation, Alren sighed and carefully opened his fisted hand for Saxon. The vampire looked on in horror at the pink petals speckled with blood that lay delicately in his hand. "Ironic isn't it. Lampocapnos means rejected love and yet everyone seeks me out to help them."

"This is why you get upset every time someone comes to you for answers," Saxon spoke the realization under his breath.

"It is not fatal for elves since we are the direct descendants of the fae and it is a fae disease. Though it is incredibly unpleasant. Some days I think that it is a wonderful thing that someone who can never catch such a curse decided to attach themselves to me, how lucky it is for you to be a vampire."

"Who is it for? How long have you had it?" The vampire pushed.

"Long before you ever pushed yourself into my life in that no-name town. Who it is for does not matter." Alren said in a steady voice, eyes vacant looking once again into the flames. "As I have told you many times now it is being handled and I will be completely fine. One way or another it will pass on its own and I will remain."

"This is why you travel so much?" He asked putting the limited information he had together in a new light.

"You can be obnoxiously observant when you wish to be." The elf sighed, closing his violet eyes. "Yes, traveling does make the symptoms easier to handle since it is harder to think of them."

"And let us not forget I am also incredibly stubborn when I wish to be as well. The morning will be a fantastic time for a visit to the healer." He initiated.

"Again Salari can do nothing but give me more tea for the pain and nausea from when it begins to act up."

"'Then that is a good reason to go, that way I can have a supply for you as well just in case. But I would like more for my own understanding of how to properly help you with this since we have no idea of when it will pass. Especially since you plan to do nothing about it I assume."

"They will never know you are correct."

"How do you contain so much venom for people who do not choose to do something about it and let themselves suffer when you do the same." Saxon huffs finally standing back up. "It makes you a hypocrite."

"I know it does considering I have the same venom for myself. The issue is I don't know why I can't let go either and I hate it some days. The feeling of being helpless to your own emotions. But through the discomfort, it will not kill me physically where it can and will kill them. Maybe through them, I can find an answer that resonates with me about why I can not let them go and let them live their lives without my selfish interference."

In the morning they left Alren's house in silence. For Saxon, it was a walk of determination but for his counterpart, it was understanding but protest. Salari would be so incredibly pissed at them both for showing up as the sun rose. He had not talked his companion out of this asinine visit. Luckily he was friendly with Salari the healer and could catch up with her once she was done cursing them for the early visit. By the time Saxon was knocking on the door, the elf was praying to any gods he could think of that she had gotten a decent night's sleep the night before, but alas his prayers were unanswered when a very disgruntled human woman threw the door open. She had obviously just woken up and had been having a trying few days if the bags under her eyes and his unkempt hair were to go by. She had just woken up if the glare she was giving the two men said anything.

"Alren Yesven what have I told you about the sun?" She hissed, sounding like more of a demon than a human woman in her mid-thirties.

"If it's not about the trees then your patience and bedmanner are still asleep and if I am not currently dying a horrible and quick death not to bother you with my elvish ass." He said with a smile standing slightly behind the much larger vampire."Though my dear Salari this endeavor is not my own, I am being dragged to you in the utmost protest and against my will by this charming behemoth who I could not dissuade." Suddenly those dark green eyes full of hatred snapped to the larger and now more terrified man.

"I do apologize, my lady, I did drag him to see you this morning more for my own peace of mind." The woman went from hostile to thoughtful within a breath giving the vampire an uneasy feeling.

"Oh is this your vampire that you are always on about? You finally brought him here? I never thought I would live to see the day. And since you are here I am assuming he knows about your little condition." She nodded, not really expecting an answer.

"He is aware and he doesn't believe me that it is handled." The man sighed.

"I am not surprised with how little care you give to your own being, how many times I have yelled at you for the same?" She sighed as well. "Come in, I have updates for you anyway."

"I am assuming they are not good updates." The elf sighed as he pushed past the raven-haired man to follow the small feisty woman inside the house.

"Have I missed something?" Saxon asked carefully, very confused about the situation.

"This arsehole and I" The woman started "Bonded over choking up flowers at the same time a few years back then proceeded to go to the tavern and drown our sorrows."

"You are also afflicted?" Saxon asked just as carefully.

"Yep he gets cough up small pink petals and I have black mush." She shrugged sitting at her small table in her kitchen motioned to the larger man to sit across from her ignoring the elf milling around behind her. He was more comfortable than Saxon expected in the woman's house.

"Alcea Rosea otherwise known as Hollyhock. Means 'please remember me' which as always is right on the nose in this situation." Alren explained to Saxon as he went into some of the cupboards to grab two mugs before going over to her kettle by the fire to pour them tea. He handed Saxon a mug before sitting beside him with his back to the window of the kitchen.

"Before you ask because everyone always does not I am not doing anything about the curse. And no I have no idea what the outcome for me will be since my darling Lyria is in fact dying of growths so there is nothing but guilt and pain waiting if I say anything."

"Honestly we don't know what will happen with a human who might outlive the person who was the reason they are afflicted. Creatures with magic in their blood have a good chance of surviving though many take their own lives in that situation." Alren added, taking a sip from his tea. "There is a good chance though unfortunate that Lyria will pass first."

"Her health is deteriorating fast Ren. And I don't think she will make it through another winter, let alone to spring." She sighed in defeat. "She began coughing up blood because of the growths and the mages say it is too far along for them to help not that she will accept the help other than mine."

"I am sorry dear, are you going to be staying with her?" Alren asked.

"Yes, well actually I have already been staying with her. Last night we had a bad emergency so I stayed in town."

"That does make the most sense." Saxon tried to add.

"Just remember our agreement, Alren." She sighed looking pointedly at the elf who just nodded.

"Of course my dear. No matter what happens you two will be sent to my estate and laid together forever." She nodded at his words before turning to a stunned Saxon. Alren's compassion always floored him.

"What do you need to know tall, dark, and honestly in over his head when involving yourself with this loveable ass." Her words caused Saxon to chuckle and relax.

"Everything about the disease and how it affects elves, please. Also, you have some tea recipes I have heard?"

"What a wonderful list. Get comfortable, we will be here awhile." She smiled.

"I will put another pot on." Alren sighed.

Story Four:
Mayflower

"Welcome"

Months had passed and the two had met with each
other multiple times on the path. Only once was a melancholy
affair. It had been late fall when he had gotten a summons to
Rysiam from the Duke himself. He had rushed across the
continent to be there for his friend as they laid Lyria and Salari
together one last time. It was a truly somber affair, he had
never seen the poet in such dark colors before. Normally he
was not as bright as a bard but grey and black were never in
his wardrobe before. Some part of Saxon truly hated seeing
the man in mourning clothes. The poet had informed the
vampire that he had been there with them as they began to
deteriorate, helping with daily chores and errands. There was a
point after Lyria had finally succumbed to the growths that
Salari might live through the loss but her body could not
handle the flowers wilting and rotting inside her and joined
her love only a few days later. It had taken Alren a few days to
call for him and handle all of their affairs before getting them
moved to his domain and his private family cemetery giving
the hunter time to get to him.

Saxon had to watch and bite his tongue as Alren
pretended not to be affected or mourn his friends in his own
home. As he swept through the halls of his manor he
supported everyone else and handled everything else. From
the burial rites and celebration of the two to grieving families

crying over the unfairness of it all. Before him was the man he had met so long ago. But this time he knew how to see past the mask of impassive determination and stone-like strength. He also had to watch as the cough came and wrecked the redhead's body any time he thought he was alone, the scent of blood on his breath more often than not. The hardest thing was no one else seemed to notice the scent or the slight tremble in the man's hands, or the grief in his eyes he couldn't quite hide.

Saxon hadn't been so quietly angry with so many strangers in a long time, though back then there was also a funeral which seemed to be an uncomfortable pattern. He would admit that Alren's sister was an amazing woman whom he could see the poet in though much more free with affection than her brother. Obviously, the closed nature was not a family trait or even a nobility trait, it was all the older man alone. The people of Rysiam were a king and welcoming people even to a strange vampire such as himself. But none of them stopped to think about their Duke and the mourning he was going through effectively alone. It was clear that he was their foundational rock but in the process his strength let them forget he is not truly made of stone. However, he kept his mouth shut and saw a different man than he knew, a different man than who walked beside him out in the middle of nowhere. This man was proper and stern yet caring and approachable. This was the Duke that was praised through the lands, the one he had heard whispers about. He was honest with himself that he missed the foul-tempered poet who was known to make people cry with words alone if they annoyed him. Or more impressively would start and finish a brawl if someone insulted something or someone he cared for, the hunter included.

"You seem bored here, I hope you know you can leave if you wish to. It was selfish to call you here for this but they have been laid to rest together already. And I am well aware there is not much to do here, especially in the winter." Alren sighed leaning against the door frame to the small private library he had shown Saxon when he had arrived. It was full of books that he had collected and refused to let leave his personal collection over the years. Saxon had been seated in one of the two overly plush and luxurious armchairs before a respectably sized fireplace.

"I am not bored just because there is nothing but peace here," Saxon reassured the elf as he sat comfortably waiting on the other to cross the threshold and join him like he normally does when the poet finds him in his private sanctuary. "There is nothing but chores and sparing waiting for me if I had gone back home this winter. Here I at the very least get to learn more about you since you realized you will not get rid of me, you left me with your sister."

"Yes, Bylar has been very open with how happy she is that you are here and what information about me she is willing to spill to you." The older man sighed pinching the bridge of his nose. The raven-haired man could see just how tired his friend was now that some of his masks were falling away.

"Oh trust me I have noticed how happy she is with you having a friend here. With all of the stories she has shared with me, especially from when you were younger. Though I must admit they have not at all enlightened me as all to why you are so closed off to everyone." He pressed honestly feeling more confident with his footing with the poet. Alren just sighed again, violet eyes still closed.

"And why pray tell, does my personality still bother you? Or my lack of open affection? Why can you not just let it go?" He said finally stepping into the room and closing the door for a moment of privacy. When he made it to the chair next to the other man he dropped down so unceremoniously Saxon thought he might have hurt himself. "You are so much more open than any other vampire I have ever met, and I have known a fair share of vampires through time."

"We are both anomalies of our cultures. I learned the hard way what happens if you hide behind fear. People die with regret and you regret something you could have fixed with a few words or actions." Saxon shrugged, setting the book he was reading down to focus on the slouching next to him.

"Yes, and I got the unfortunate lesson on the opposite side of the spectrum. I learned what happens if those open affections are misplaced. If they are treated as nothing but a burden." The elf admitted closing his eyes again.

"What do you mean? Who could have rejected you?" Saxon asked, completely appalled. "The loyalty and affection of an elf aside why would anyone tell you that your feelings were a burden? You are clever and creative with a sharp wit and a sharper tongue that would make advisors in court swoon."

"Many people would Saxon." His tone made the vampire freeze in the chair, and coldness in his bones set in even this close to the fire. "In my long life, I have had this curse multiple times and each has been truly unreceptive hence my unwillingness to try again." He admitted. "My first time I was a child coughing up yellow carnations meaning rejection and unwanted. I began reading about flowers at 188 years old to try to understand what was happening. I studied everything I could about the flowers and this damn curse. I was 190 when my heart was truly broken for the first time and

I poured everything into the ink I was given to 'sort myself out like a gentleman'."

"You were so young." Saxon was almost beside himself unable to contain the storm of feelings inside him. The vacant look in the elf's eyes was not helping the fear clawing up the vampire's throat.

"Did you know in rare cases you can get flowers platonically or in even fewer cases familial ties can cause it as well?" He answered instead, his voice completely flat.

"I have heard in my research yes." He knew that the elf knew he had been trying to find all the information he could on the disease since he found out the elf was inflicted.

"My mother never wanted my father. She married him for his title, it was a business transaction. And I was the product of that transaction. I know my father loves me and he tried, no tries, to shield me from it all the best he could. He couldn't hide it when she was pregnant with Blyar. It is no secret that Blyar is technically my half-sister though we never talk about it. The way she very obviously loved her before she was born was enough to trigger my first encounter. She laughed at me and said my flowers were right, I was unwanted. My father cried for me. It was shortly after Blyar was born that I went to a mage alone and in secret, I remember being so afraid. The mage told me that I wouldn't die but this was no way for a boy to live. He helped me through when I was alone and feeling empty. Luckily it never affected my relationship with Blyar even if she was the trigger. My mother either never noticed or never cared. I think my father knows but could never bring himself to confirm."

"How many times?" Saxon asked in a broken whisper that crawled from the pain in his chest.

"Not including the first and now I have had this curse seventeen times. Six trips to a mage and ten deaths. Two passed on their own as the feelings waned naturally and this one will pass or they will die first as much as I hate to admit it."

"What about the mage?"

"Those are for the times that it was caused by immortals that I can not escape like my mother or a vampire who was chosen to marry another after a sordid affair."

"That is how you knew so much about vampires when we met the first time." Things began making sense that had always been a mystery.

"You are not the first I have traveled with. Though you are the first in a few centuries."

"And none had a semblance of a happy ending did they?"

"Oh each did have a happy ending, do not worry about that. I was just not a part of their happy endings." He answered rolling his head to see his companion with a gaze that would haunt the vampire for the rest of his days. Those normally bright violet eyes lacked not only their spark of life but the fight he adored so much. He never wanted to see the poet's eyes so dull ever again.

"No one else here knows do they?" Realizing no one seemed worried about him here might have been more pressing than he originally thought. If no one knew of course no one would be worried.

"Salari knew, the healer here knows and so does the mage. You are the only other who knows in this world. My father doesn't even know about the others, only the first." He looked back into the fire. "The rest have been hidden from all until you." He admitted. "At this point in my life, what would I gain from exposing myself. Each time so far has been truly unreciprocated, each a was a clear message that whatever affection I have tends to be unwelcome in whatever capacity." He shrugged. "When you are constantly reminded of the fact your affection is not welcome to those who you care about is not welcome you stop showing any. It is easier to get called an unfeeling bastard than to have it used against me again and again. What is the point if all it brings is pain?"

"So you push people away before they can hurt you. Which is why you were so surprised when I pushed back to stay or how concerned I was about your health and safety," Saxon added.

"Observant as always in the most inconvenient ways."

"Am I the only one you are ever truly yourself with anymore?" The raven-haired man asked, ignoring the comment.

"It would seem so." He sighed looking at the vampire. "And what a miserable being you have to deal with, well until you leave as everyone else has." He said as if talking about an inevitability.

"Do not count me out so soon poet." He spoke knowing that his words would not truly reach the poet but hoping nonetheless that they would help pull him from the hole he was spiraling into. "Instead of killing me off early in your head, how about you show me outside these manor walls. Maybe we both have been cooped up too long in these walls for the melancholy to have taken hold of us like this."

"Fine if you are going to be insistent though I was not killing you off in my mind just so you know." The elf sighed standing knowing the tone of the vampire's voice only left room for pestering if he was left ignored.

"I know what was playing in your mind but death is the only way I would stay away. You may not believe me now but eventually you will." He replied with not an ounce of uncertainty as he stretched standing from the chair he had been sitting in for much too long. Maybe a walk in the fresh cold winter air was just what he needed. What they both needed to clear their minds.

"Do not hold your breath. Time has proven again and again that trust is a dangerous thing." The elf retorted watching the larger man readjust himself.

Not even an hour had passed before the men were bundled and strolling the stone streets of the city of Rysiam. Snow was falling around them. People had kept stopping their rush to get ready for the winter festival to greet the redhead much to Saxon's amusement. Even children ran up to them excitedly, with no fear at all for their Duke. One memorable moment was the little girl handing the man a flower before giggling and running off.

"Hellebore means peace, serenity, and tranquility to most but it can also mean stress and anxiety," Alren spoke automatically into the air like he could not withhold the information if he wanted to.

"Sounds like change for the better or the path to it don't you think Mr. Poet?"

"For a bounty hunter, you are so optimistic all the time."

"One of us has to be. Now I see a bakery and I know lemon cakes are your favorite so let us head over. You have had enough dark thoughts to warrant some sweetness to balance." He dragged the grumbling smaller man into the small bakery he saw across the street. It was a cute little shop Saxon thought, the baker herself was cheerfully talking to two women who had already been inside when they entered.

"I will be right with you." The incredibly tiny woman called over as they began to browse her selection.

"Take your time we are looking around," Saxon called back, neither were in a rush but their entrance seemed to have broken whatever atmosphere had been there before between the three women. Soon enough the vampire watched the other customers say their farewells, each taking a chance to place a swift kiss on one of the baker's cheeks before leaving quickly with identical smiles on their faces. They left a brightly-faced woman behind with a blush spreading across her face deep enough to rival the poet's hair. It was a truly sweet moment until the coughing began shaking the poor woman left behind, the violent spasms causing her to brace against the wall behind her in case she lost her balance and hurt herself further. Saxon cursed to any god who would listen under his breath as he rushed to her, holding her weight before she could slide to the ground, coughs still wrecking her body. He knew what it was the moment he smelled the faint twinge of blood in the air and cursed their luck. He wanted Alren to escape this for a little bit, not run into more. He carefully held onto her making sure to support her little bit of weight as the flowers finally came out and spewed on the floor of her bakery.

"Mayflowers." Alren sighed examining the petals that had fallen from her.

"My Lord?" She asked tensing, finally realizing who was kneeling beside her.

"I am going to take an educated guess and assume these are for at least one of the women who was just here with you if not both of them." He raised a brow looking back at her.

"Yes sir, both if I can be honest but I only have one flower." She said quietly.

"What is your name?" He asked, sounding gentle and tired.

"Mikla my Lord." She refused to look him in the eyes, her gaze bouncing from her own flowers to just beside him but never directly at him.

"And their names?" He pressed.

"Claria and Malia. They were born and raised here in Rysiam, and have been married many years. I met them sometime back after moving here and opening my store. They have come in weekly since that first visit to spend time saying they have never had such goods before. Even if it is a lie it is nice to hear." She smiles with an air of longing.

"Understandable to feel that way, it is hard when people who you grow to care about make such large comments like that. It can be hard to believe even if it is their truth. Though I believe you should talk to them." Alren sighed. "Even before looking at your flowers, I can tell they are interested in more than just your baking. But for a bit of peace of mind, Mayflowers mean welcome, as in to welcome someone in. You can have happiness."

"Is that really alright my Lord? For me to want two people? Three people together? Isn't that greedy for me to want such a thing?" She asked finally, looking her deep brown eyes into his violet asking something that obviously gnawed at her for some time.

"Love is not something that is greedy, not in the way man is. When it is the pure feeling of admiration and affection it is not greedy. Some people have more love than one other person can handle. That being said if you are not hurting anyone it doesn't matter what others think of it. Just be happy. That is all I ask of my people."

"Thank you, my Lord." She whispered, tears welling in her eyes. His words must have been the ones she had been waiting desperately to hear. Permission to be happy. Saxon had a fleeting thought about the unfairness that Alren could give permission to others to find happiness but for some reason, he could not give it to himself.

"Do not thank me for something anyone who cares about any of you would say." He groaned standing back up.

"You truly care about us all don't you?" She asked less scared to talk to the redhead directly.

"Of course I do, you all rely on me." He shrugged like his words were a small unimportant thing. "Though I think it is time to return to the manor. It seems I am reaching my limit on interaction today."

"Of course Alren. I didn't mean for us to get caught right back in the same situation. Let us get you some cakes and then we can go back to your library and hide away." Saxon apologized, helping the woman back to her feet before letting go and stepping back to the elf. "At least in Salari's memory, you have led a path for Mikla to be happy." He tried knowing this had not been the best outcome.

"My Lord?" She asked confused and curious.

"My apologies, we just laid a friend to rest with her partner. She did not make it through her partner's passing due to poor health. We had hoped that the flowers would not take her as well but she could not handle it. We just said our final farewells just a bit ago." Saxon explained. The woman looked between the men in shock and sorrow.

"Oh, my dear. My condolences to you both. And here you are helping me while you are grieving." She pushed away from Saxon to rush around the shop with a new wind. Collecting various items and setting them on the counter. She finally stopped a moment to pack the goods in a basket before shoving the treats into Saxon's arms. "I will not take no for an answer. Take them. Sweets help with sadness. Just promise me you will take care of our Lord for us." She spoke sternly pointing a finger at the larger man's chest.

"Of course I will." He answered without a thought. She just smiled at him as Alren shook his head. However, he did not disagree with the notion of the vampire taking care of him this time.

Story Five:
Crocus

"Youthful joy, love, abuse not"

When one is centuries old, time tends to fly by with the birds. They walked together for over two years before Saxon learned something about the curse that made him rush to find his friend with pure terror pushing him. He had been across the continent on an early spring contract, much earlier in the year than he would leave to find the poet but he had no time to spare with what he had learned. It took him longer than he would have liked to track him down in some other no-name town just like those years ago.

He walked into the tavern to see the poet safe and reading to the crowd. Each person around him was completely enraptured with him, once he had joked about siren blood in his ancestry only for the elf to feign insult and threaten to make him sleep on the floor of their room. What kept him in the shadows instead of stepping to his poet was the bard strumming next to him creating an ambiance. He stood and watched from a shrouded corner for a moment before his friend noticed him. Very rarely could he be an unknown fan in the crowd, even during an unplanned meeting the elf would pick him from wherever he hid. The bard beside him had yet to notice though that he too was being watched by what many would count as a predator. He was clearly another elven man but much younger than the poet, stark white hair was much more common than Alren's red. His eyes were a mesmerizing blue that reminded the hunter of a pool of clear water on a summer's day. The biggest difference between the two artists though was the relaxed demeanor of the bard and the lazy smile. He was the free-loving creature one would expect from an elf. He could not deny even to himself that they were a striking pair performing together.

The bard was strolling around the crowd that gathered, gaining open affection as he passed strangers, so much different than the stationary poet who calmly stepped away only to move out of someone's reach as they got too close. The younger man was clearly thriving in the attention as he strummed his lute along, perfectly matching Alren as he spoke his written words.

"Darling we have a very intent and dangerous fan." the elven musician whispered to the poet as the last notes faded from the air. As carefully as he could he tried to point his head without drawing attention to the vampire. Saxon could only assume he was trying not to draw attention to the fact he noticed the hunter watching them intently not knowing he could hear them over the excitement and mummers.

"Not a fan Auren just a lurker who has to make himself a nuisance." The poet spoke in the most deadpan voice he could, Saxon knew that voice was meant in teasing even if the other elf did not.

"Excuse me lordling but I would count myself a fan, your biggest fan even." He teased back as smoothly as he possibly could. No one stopped him as he walked into the poet's space, not even the bard whose eyes went wide at the sound of his voice.

"Where have you been hiding this man?" The lighter elf almost squeaked causing Saxon to wince at the volume and pitch. "Did you hear that voice? And look at him, the definition of tall, dark, and mysterious."

"Calm yourself Auren. Saxon does not know how to deal with your kind of personality and I doubt he wants his ears to bleed in your excitement." Alren sighed, finally turning his full attention to the raven.

"And what could you possibly mean by that?" The other elf squeaked again in offense.

"You are an elven bard, what else do I need to say for you to understand?" Alren smirked. "Hello Saxon, you seem more tired than normal. When was the last time you have eaten?"

"You have made a new friend, Alren?" He asked ignoring the question, his eating habits had come into question recently and Saxon did not know how he would react if Alren actually offered him some of his blood. The vampire instead chuckled as the poet wrinkled his nose at the accusation.

"Oh and his laugh, you are a horrible man for not sharing him with me before." Came a whine from the forgotten elf.

"He is not a friend but a fungus who will not leave me be, though for you that must sound familiar." Alren groaned to himself dramatically.

"Yes, you used to say that about me. Does that mean I have made it from growth to something more?" He teased. "Because I know by now you care for me and I will never let you deny it again."

"Something like that." He sighed with a small content smile. "Though this one decided for himself that my poetry needed a song list to go with it when it was read aloud. He has been here nonstop since we left the academy this past spring. He latched onto me while I was teaching and has not let go since, he even followed me home to Rysiam to handle everything."

"Ah, so you have a newly minted bond as a barker. Exactly what you wanted deep in your heart." Saxon teased again.

"Oh, you think you know my inner workings so well Mr. Hunter? Do not get jealous, you brute you are still my favorite annoyance." Alren smiled at the vampire with a mischievous fire in his eyes. Auren watched the scene unfold with curiosity and shock.

"I am glad to know I have not been replaced. Especially since I had to come looking for you." Saxon sighed with just as much dramatics. "And you have been here making art with a younger man."

"Oh, I would not call what we have been doing art," Auren interjected, wiggling his eyebrows.

"Ignore him, that is what I do. Now Saxon what did you need to have you tracking me down like I was your mark. It is barely summer and we normally wouldn't meet for another few weeks normally." He asked curious but not upset to see the other man.

"Before we talk are you done with your set for the evening?" He asked.

"I am done but worry not Auren has a set to do by himself this evening. I have my own room if we need to talk in private."

"Well, I will need a room tonight anyway." Saxon winked, causing Auren to groan again. "If you don't mind sharing a room with me once more."

"Only if you don't mind sharing a bed like we normally do." He answered with a raised brow in challenge. Auren continued to watch on with wide eyes at both men, not knowing where to take their comments or what questions to ask them.

"Oh you know I have never had an issue sharing a bed with you, not since that awkward first time." He smirked, enjoying the youngest elf's reactions. "I shall follow you to your room."

"Auren go enjoy your set. I will see you for dinner later on." Alren said with a stern tone that left no room for discussion or any questions about what would happen if they were interrupted. When the bard nodded without saying a word the poet spun around and left with a certainty that the hunter was a step behind. Once the climb up the stairs and the walk down the hall to the third door was done without a single word was completed they continued on into the room, closing the door still without a sound. It wasn't until the room was sealed off to the outside world did the smaller man finally turned back to the larger man. Saxon knew that Alren was watching him closely, watching him fidget like he always does when he is nervous. "What is wrong Saxon?" He asked carefully, becoming concerned with his friend's behavior.

"I learned something a few weeks ago on a contract that I needed to share with you." The vampire spoke carefully not knowing how to bring this up now that he was face to face with the redhead.

"What did you learn that has you so scared to speak to me?" He stepped closer very slowly like Saxon was a frightened animal.

"I was talking to an elven mage and you know I always check for new information for your infliction. I always try to find something new for you and those you help." He started.

"Yes, I know you are gentle-hearted and stubborn on the subject of the disease of flowers and those who suffer with it." Alren nodded along.

"This elven mage had information specifically for elves with the affliction. You are not the only one who has been afflicted this many times in their long lives." He continues.

"At least I am not the only one cursed to live a life alone." Alren sighed.

"You are not alone but that is also not the issue." Saxon sighed. "We know that the disease barely affects you. The issue is when it happens too often in elves or even fae their body finally gives out and in the end, it can kill you because their body can not handle the flowers anymore." Saxon stressed his words watching Alren think about the situation.

"So it can kill me? Having my heart broken too many times can kill me? My unwanted feelings could kill me like it does everyone else." Alren said in shock.

"Does Auren know you have it?" He asked quietly.

"No, he does not, no one new knows about it," Alren said, lost in thought.

"We don't know when your body could give out due to all the stress." He tried to push the seriousness of the situation. "You need to tell them or go to a mage if you think that it has no hope of reciprocation. You have not been allowed to let it pass in all the years I have known you. You might put too much stress on your body holding it in and it could start to give out. We might not even have the time to let the feelings pass on their own or let them live their lives." That seemed to pull Alren's attention back to the vampire.

"I will be fine Saxon. If it kills me then it kills me and I will be out of my misery finally." That sent a shiver down Saxon's spine and fear chilling his bones.

"Alren are you planning on letting this kill you?" He asked in a whispered tone.

"No, I am not planning on letting it kill me, I never planned on letting it kill me," Alren said calmly letting Saxon release a breath he didn't know he was holding in. "But I won't stop it either. If I am lucky this will be my last time dealing with this curse all together."

"How could you once again be so flippant about your health?" He blurted out. "I thought we were past this."

"Saxon I need you to understand I am tired. These petals just continue to prove how unwanted I am. I am tired of thinking things are going well just to cough up flowers over feelings I don't want." Alren sighed looking his entire age for once. So weary, so tired, so broken. "I am not being flippant, I am tired of fighting. You know elves aren't supposed to be alone and here I am."

"You know that none of these have been your fault and if these people can not see what they have with you then they are not worth your affection," Saxon said not thinking he would actually get a reply.

"Something has to be wrong with me if this keeps happening, Saxon if I keep ending up alone." He replied, sounding so tired, the larger man absolutely hated it. If only he could protect his poet from everything, including the carelessness that others were handling his well-being and emotions.

"You are not alone, not anymore." The I am here was heard loud and clear even though it was unsaid.

"You don't travel with me all the time. And eventually, Auren will go off on his own." Alren sighed acting like this was a given fact of life.

"Do not count the kid out yet. And if you wanted me to all you would have to do is ask and I will travel with you all the time. We can find ways to deal with contracts and competitions that conflict with each other."

"You would really be willing to do that for me?" The elf seemed genuinely surprised.

"Of course, I would. I can't make things change with your humans but you are no longer alone. You haven't been in years. Not since the first time I followed you. I will even travel with a bard for you." He teased.

"You know this won't fix everything." The elf pushed.

"I know that won't fix everything but at least until we can fix the flowers it should help. I hope it is enough to help you fight through, and I wish I could promise it will be the last time but I don't know the future."

"You still want me to tell them, don't you? Or go to a mage." Alren sighed, still staring at the vampire like he was reading him as easily as he would a book.

"I would prefer it, yes but I have said nothing since that night after we laid Salari and Lyria to rest together," Saxon admitted. He had wanted to discuss it so many times over the years. But he couldn't bring himself to as he saw Alren breathe easier after that winter. He had hoped maybe it would pass but every now and again it would come back up.

"I know. You are a strange one wearing your emotions on your sleeve out in the open like nothing can hurt you."

"You have never seen me deal with others when I do not care about them or want to make a decent impression on them." The vampire shrugged. He was told he was an unholy bastard by a lot of people, a cold unfeeling person.

"Fair enough I guess," Alren smirked.

"I have told you before I have too much regret over things being left unsaid," Saxon replied.

"One day you will tell me your stories. For someone so open with your emotions your past still remains a secret to me still." Alren said with his head tilted in curiosity.

"I will give you all my secrets the moment that the last flowers fall from your lips." Saxon challenged. "That way you have something to look forward to."

"Then I have no choice." Alren sighed dramatically. "I must attempt to persevere in the pursuit of knowledge and curiosity." Saxon just laughed uncontrollably at his antics.

"Come on you brute let us go check on our bard less he gets swept away."

"Well I mean I don't think we need a pet bard," Saxon says, catching his breath finally.

"Yes but now we have one to take care of and if you are sticking around it makes him your responsibility as well. He is not a pet, more like a child."

"You do know normally we would get a pet then before a child together." Saxon raised his brow in amusement.

"Normally we would be in a relationship before getting a pet or a child bard but here we are."

"You don't consider our years of commitment to each other a relationship?" Saxon quipped. "Alren I am highly offended." He gasped.

"Considering we have a bard now. If you want a relationship I want a proper courting to prove your commitment." Alren teased. "I am a Duke, not some hussy that you can leave in some tavern with our bard to frolic off."

"Well of course my lord. Only the best a hunter can provide for you both." Saxon teased back watching Alren step around him towards the door.

"Set your things down so that we can go back down unless you have something more we need to talk about." The elf gestured back to the other wall across from the bed waiting for the vampire to unload everything he had traveled with.

By the time they finally made it back down to the sitting area in the tavern. They found their bard with a young man at a table. They had obviously been chatting while waiting for the bard's set. Something had quite clearly made the bard upset as tears rolled down his face as he watched the brunette man across from him. Both older men walked faster across the floor toward the younger men.

"Auren, what is wrong? Are you alright?" Alren said with clear genuine concern in his voice once they were in earshot. The bard looked up with bright eyes and a red blotchy face.

"Alren this poor boy has the flowers." The bard's voice was thick with emotion as Saxon groaned behind the redhead.

"Every gods damned time." Saxon began to rub his temples. How do these situations always end up following them everywhere?

"Every time." The poet sighed agreeing. "Alright boy, show me your flowers." The man said in a stern tone turning to the human male at the table. The candlelight in the tavern made the man seem sickly in complexion. Dark eyes looked up at him in shock before holding out a purple flower in his shaking hand. "Crocus they do mean youthful joy, love, abuse not."

"You are him, aren't you. The poet who knows all about the flowers. The Duke who travels and helps people afflicted." The young man's eyes went wide in recognition. The bard watched on with wide eyes putting things together from rumors he had heard before of the Duke who knew everything about the disease, and here he was with the legend. Saxon watched the realizations cross his face with a very small amount of amusement.

"Yes I am, that is not the important part here. Do you know who the flowers are for?" Alren slid past the recognition.

"Yes of course Sir. They are for two of my fellow guards. We started at the same time and made a squad with each other to patrol. I do know they have flowers for each other. I have been trying to convince both to talk to each other so that they could be happy and to have faith in each other.

"Take your own advice and talk to both of them. However, if they would like I will be here until after the bard's set to be able to check their flowers as well. I will be able to give them some peace of mind if nothing else." The human nodded excitedly before rushing out of the tavern floor. Auren wiped his face clearing away the tears as he watched the human rush out.

"You are too kind sometimes, my lordling," Saxon whispered in the poet's ear from his spot behind him. They only stood a breath apart as the bard watched on. The younger man finally shook his head and began rubbing his face to try to get himself ready for his set.

"Not everyone has to suffer." The poet uttered quietly leaning back against the hunter. Neither wanted the bard to overhear them, especially the suffer like I do.

The night continued on like nothing had ever happened like things tend to. While Auren performed his set, dancing around the tavern and singing his songs. Sometime after Alren had eaten and while he and Saxon were sitting at the table the guard returned with two other human men in tow. The two men they had yet to meet were not nearly as excited as the one dragging them. Once the introductions were made the two other guards finally understood why the first had brought them here. Finally, they handed over the flowers, surprised when they each had the same crocus'. Alren watched as they all hugged and laughed through tears as they realized what this meant. They held onto each other for strength and belief. Alren watched them with a longing look. He just looked back at the vampire and gave a small smile before watching the guards excuse themselves. The elf just continued to watch those around them.

Saxon watched the red-headed elf with a knot in his chest and questions in his mind. Something about the lighting and atmosphere made it almost impossible for the hunter to take his eyes off of the poet, even with the bard bouncing around the room and the loud conversations going on around them. Thoughts like these were hard enough without traveling together all the time. How long could he go without letting anything slip?

See you next Novella November for Part Two

www.ingramcontent.com/pod-product-compliance
Lightning Source LLC
Chambersburg PA
CBHW040836010625
27395CB00010B/40